DEATH OF A
TELENOVELA STAR

DEATH OF A TELENOVELA STAR

TERESA DOVALPAGE

THORNDIKE PRESS
A part of Gale, a Cengage Company

GALE
A Cengage Company

LIBRARY OF CONGRESS CIP DATA ON FILE.
CATALOGUING IN PUBLICATION FOR THIS BOOK
IS AVAILABLE FROM THE LIBRARY OF CONGRESS.

ISBN-13: 978-1-4328-8756-8 (hardcover alk. paper)

Published in 2021 by arrangement with Soho Press, Inc.

Printed in Mexico
Print Number: 01   Print Year: 2021

To Staci Matlock, muchas gracias for your encouragement!

1: SHENANIGANS

Aboard the *North Star* were five thousand travelers and one open bar. What could be expected from such a crowd but shenanigans? That's what Marlene Martínez thought as she looked around her with suspicion. With so many passengers crammed onto the one-thousand-foot boat, something bad was bound to happen.

Her grandfather, bless his soul, used to say, "Somewhere, something bad is happening to somebody right now." Years ago, Marlene had laughed at his unabashed pessimism, but now, watching from her lounge chair the noisy throng waiting by the pool for their cabins to be ready, she couldn't avoid a sense of dread.

Something bad is going to happen to somebody on this ship.

It was the first cruise Marlene had ever taken. A short one, just seven days' roundtrip from Miami to Belize, Costa

Maya and Cozumel. Though she had initially booked the trip on impulse for her niece, Sarita, as a *quinceañera* present, she'd found herself anticipating a fun, relaxing vacation. But there was something in the air. A hint of danger that, as a former detective, Marlene knew too well.

Sarita was celebrating her fifteenth birthday that month, and the only thing she wanted was to get away from "Culo del Mundo." She lived in Albuquerque, a city that Marlene agreed was the rear end of the world. Sarita screamed and hugged her aunt when she heard about her present, saying a Caribbean cruise sounded "sick."

The trip was also a reward for Sarita, who had stayed out of trouble after a rough start that year, a shoplifting incident at the Coronado mall and what her father — Marlene's brother — called "the pot *problemita.*" She had been caught smoking dope in the schoolyard with her best friends, Lupe and Jane, and all three of the girls had been suspended for two weeks and sent to a counselor. "The others were the instigators," her father told Marlene. "It was peer pressure." But the girls were all careful to stay on their best behavior afterwards. They started an online newspaper for their journalism class and ran articles about Latino nights at The Cooperage — a popular Albuquerque steakhouse — hiking the La Luz trail in the Sandia Mountains, and the state's incentives for the film industry in New Mexico.

Sarita loved being a reporter so much, she'd taken a two-month internship at the *Albuquerque Journal.* She deserved a reward, and Marlene was happy to provide one. But just in case, Sarita's mother had cautioned her sister-in-law to keep the girl on a short leash for the duration of the cruise.

That wouldn't be easy, though. Just before boarding, Marlene had found out that Carloalberto, a part-time model and aspiring actor from Cuba who went by only his first name, was among the passengers. It wasn't uncommon to find celebrities on these short Caribbean cruises, particularly when those celebrities were C-listers, as Carloalberto happened to be. Besides starring in several telenovelas, he had been made almost famous by his appearance on *The Terrific Two,* a TV program that featured actor-screenwriter pairs competitively pitching their movie ideas to Hollywood producers. The winning team would receive enough funding for their proposed project. They were down to the last round, and Carloalberto and his partner, a screenwriter

9

named Helen Hall, were among the three teams left.

Marlene had never heard of them. Her Miami bakery, La Bakería Cubana, kept her too busy to watch much TV. But Sarita hadn't stopped talking about Carloalberto since she'd arrived in Miami. She even showed Marlene headshots of him that she for some reason had on her phone, so her aunt couldn't quite ignore his presence. He was tanned and tall, in his early twenties with gym-rat muscles, a chiseled jaw and what Sarita described as "a kissable mouth."

And here he was, a few feet from Marlene. She looked for her niece, but the girl wasn't around, so she allowed herself time to admire the man — just for fun, of course. He was far too young to take seriously, and Marlene hadn't yet recovered from her last love affair, which had ended quite poorly — though she supposed it could have been much worse. Still, she could admit that Carloalberto was a handsome specimen, although there was something alarmingly familiar about him. What was it?

He was talking to an older blond man in a Hawaiian shirt. After exchanging a few words, the two of them walked behind the pool bar where a frazzled bartender chain-served mojitos and daiquiris. They seemed to want to hide from the fray. Marlene watched their mouths. In her time on the Cuban police force, she had learned to read lips. It helped that their conversation was in Spanish.

"I don't have it yet," Carloalberto said, his well-defined jaw shaking. "You'll have to wait until the show is over."

"How do we know you're going to win?" the other replied. "There's no guarantee those Hollywood *pendejos* don't get rid of you tomorrow."

"They won't. I promise! As a finalist, I practically have that money secured."

"Practically won't cut it."

"Please, be patient. I've always come through before, haven't I?"

"Yes, but now you're late. I'm not a patient man."

"Look, I had a source of income that's . . . no longer available. But I have money coming my way. Please, just give me a month."

The man eyed him carefully.

"You get a week," he said through clenched teeth. "One. If you don't come up with something by the time the cruise ends, you're in trouble. Got it?"

Carloalberto nodded. His perfect tan looked slightly paler. Mr. Hawaiian Shirt left. Carloalberto stayed motionless, staring at the Miami lights shimmering along the coastline as the boat sailed out to sea.

Marlene had been so focused on the exchange that she didn't realize Sarita was there until the girl grabbed her arm.

"Did you see him, Tía?" She pointed to Carloalberto. "That's the one I've been telling you about! Isn't he the most beautiful *papichuli* in the world? I can't believe we're going to spend a whole week on the same boat as him! Do you think he'll notice me?"

"I hope not, *mijita.*"

Sarita whipped out her smartphone, which had a pink case covered in glitter. She punched in a number and started talking a mile a minute. It surprised Marlene. Her niece seldom used her phone to make calls — only to text and send WhatsApp messages.

Shenanigans are brewing, thought Marlene.

2: SUNDOWN AT SEA

The ship was traveling at around twenty knots, or twenty-three miles, per hour, the cruise channel informed passengers. The Miami coastline was no longer visible. The casino and the onboard boutiques, which had been closed while in port, opened their doors and welcomed the herd of passengers that rushed to them right away.

Marlene and Sarita's stateroom was located on deck fourteen, mid-ship. The girl let out a happy cry when she saw it.

"Aww, Tía, I didn't expect it to be so nice!"

The cabin had two sofa beds, a dresser, an armchair and a spacious closet with enough room for their luggage. Marlene had packed a pair of jeans, a few shorts and T-shirts, one formal just-in-case outfit and a bathing suit, but Sarita carried in her two backpacks dresses, shirts, skirts, bikinis and tankinis; in sum, more clothes than days the cruise was going to last.

The cabin had generally been designed to make the most of minimal space, but also had a few nice touches, like prints of tropical birds and butterflies in blue metal frames on the walls and a pretty glass carafe and two cups on a silver tray over the minibar.

The shower had a translucent frosted glass door. North Star–branded cotton bathrobes and slippers sat nearby on a lacquered shelf.

"On *fleek,*" Sarita concluded.

Marlene hoped that meant she liked it.

A round table and two green mesh chairs furnished the balcony. The stateroom was a deck above the lifeboats, which Marlene appreciated, since they would have obstructed a stunning ocean view.

After unpacking, they went out and spent the next fifteen minutes deciding where to eat. It shouldn't have been a difficult choice, considering that the two main dining rooms, dubbed "Delicious" and "Scrumptious," served exactly the same menu. There was also a buffet spot, The Forest Café, but it was crowded.

Marlene suggested Delicious, which was on deck seven and had a ten-minute wait time according to the electronic sign above its door. But when Sarita spotted Carloalberto outside The Ambassador — a specialty restaurant with a fifteen-dollar surcharge per person for entrance — she insisted on eating there despite its having triple the wait time. After some back and forth, Marlene relented, though it meant they had to go back to the cabin and change — the restaurant had a dress code. Truthfully, though, she was still intrigued by the earlier exchange between the aspiring actor and the blond in the Hawaiian shirt.

When they entered the restaurant, Sarita wowed softly at the flowing red curtains and gold-plated mirrors. A small art gallery of Impressionist paintings covered one wall. Their tuxedoed waiter led them to a white-clothed table for two and promptly brought over bread in a silver basket — warm rolls, focaccia and garlic knots. Marlene was presented with an encyclopedic wine list but ordered a modest Zinfandel. Italian music played in the background.

"This is Verdi's *La Traviata*," Sarita said.

"Really?" Marlene asked, surprised. "How do you know?"

"When I was interning at the *Journal*, the editor I was working with did a feature on the Santa Fe Opera," the girl explained with a self-satisfied look. "They even gave us free tickets. I learned a ton about classical music there."

"Well, I'm proud of you!"

Carloalberto was sitting by himself at a table for four, dressed in a dark blue suit and tie. Formality forgotten, Sarita retrieved her cell phone and entered a password. Marlene was looking at her niece's manicured nails, painted a bright green, and noticed that she had typed in a series of 2s to unlock her phone. *Coño,* could the girl not have chosen a more secure passcode? Sarita started snapping pictures of the actor as discreetly as she could, which was not very discreetly. He didn't seem to notice, or maybe he was used to it.

"I can't wait to send these to Jane and Lupe!" Sarita said. "And post them on Instagram for all my ABQ friends. They'll be so jealous!"

Marlene made her stop. Sarita was practically about to throw a tantrum, but when a tall, well-dressed woman joined Carloalberto, the girl shut up immediately. The woman was a stunning leggy brunette with green eyes.

"That's his wife, Emma," Sarita said in a reverent tone. "She's a model, half-Venezuelan and half-Italian. She's so skinny and beautiful! Ah, I wish I looked like her, but I'm saddled with this big butt." Sarita sulked.

Marlene wanted to lecture her on self-esteem and body image, but what good would it do? Besides, most teenagers had image issues and outgrew them along with acne.

They ate quietly. Sarita kept eyeing the couple and sighing. Carloalberto and his wife didn't talk much either. The model, as Sarita pointed out, looked annoyed.

For dessert, Marlene ordered Baked Alaska. She was enjoying the pairing of vanilla ice cream and warm meringue when Sarita jumped in her chair. Another woman had showed up at the couple's table.

"This ship is chock-full of celebrities!" the girl whispered. "Do you know who she is?"

Marlene glanced at the newcomer. She was thirty-something, slightly chubby, with brown hair and a mousy expression.

"No idea," she answered, turning her attention to the sponge cake.

"Helen, his screenwriting partner on the show! I think she has a crush on Carloalberto. But I mean, who doesn't? Look how she's kissing him!"

It certainly wasn't the usual cheek-to-cheek air kiss. Hers was lingering, longer than Latino social greeting protocol dictated. The model didn't say a word as Carloalberto and Helen chatted away.

"Ese huevo quiere sal," said Marlene.

"What eggs, Tía? What needs salt?"

"It's what you say when somebody is coming onto someone else," Marlene explained.

"Of course Helen's into him, but she has no chance," Sarita said. "She's so average-looking, or even below that next to Emma!"

After dinner, Sarita followed Carloalberto and the two women to the casino on the same deck. Marlene grudgingly followed, not daring to leave her niece alone for one second with these troublesome celebrities.

"Isn't there enough to do on this ship for you not to stalk these people?" she grumbled.

"I'm not *stalking* anybody. I'm just walking around! I've never been inside a casino before."

To Marlene's surprise, many of the slot machines were already taken.

"How silly, to pay this much just to park yourself in front of a screen," she said.

More serious players had gathered around a craps table, Carloalberto and Helen among them. The guy in the Hawaiian shirt sauntered around, stopping here and there to observe a round or test out a slot machine. But he always kept an eye on the actor, who seemed well aware of his presence. His hands shook whenever he took a chip from the tall stack before him. Not far from there, Emma was absorbed in a baccarat game.

Marlene left Sarita circling Carloalberto — there were other teenage girls doing the same — and visited the closest boutique. She bought a straw hat since she had forgotten to pack hers, a yellow tunic dress with the North Star logo, and a bottle of suntan lotion. Then she took the elevator to leave her purchases in the cabin before picking Sarita up. They had tickets for the Blue Man Group that night.

The elevator door opened. Carloalberto was inside, admiring his reflection in the mirrored side panel in a way that Marlene found gag-worthy. At close range, he was less handsome. His eyes were small, beady and too close together, and his forehead unnaturally smooth and shiny, revealing a recent encounter with Botox. He got off on deck twelve.

Once in her stateroom, Marlene placed her purchases in the closet and her wallet in the safety box. She had brought a few La Bakería Cubana business cards. She didn't anticipate needing them there, but you never know when a new investor or chef might wander by. This bakery was her most ambitious undertaking, inspired by sampling far too many mediocre offerings in town, and she was determined to make it big.

A splendid sundown ignited the horizon in red and orange hues. Marlene walked to the balcony, and a salty mist enveloped her like a lace scarf. Other passengers were also outside enjoying the view, but not all were interested in the beauty of nature. There was a couple making out on the balcony diagonally below theirs. The man was Carloalberto, and the woman was his plain-looking screenwriter.

Wait till I tell Sarita, Marlene thought. *Sometimes being beautiful isn't enough.*

But hadn't Carloalberto left the elevator on deck twelve? That meant he should have been two decks below, not one.

Suddenly, he pushed his partner away and hurried inside the cabin. Marlene wondered if Emma had walked in. She hoped so.

3: A Duplex in Bacuranao

"Men cause more trouble than they are worth," Marlene whispered to herself as the memory resurged.

It was the day her life fell apart, scattering tender pieces of her heart in every direction. In the ocean mist, she saw Yoel the painter. The beach bum. The *hijoeputa* she could have killed when she found out.

Marlene and Yoel had been together only seven months, but she had fallen hard. He had moved in with her after her mother's death — a vulnerable moment in her life, she realized too late. He had been pleading with her to do a *permuta,* a house swap, from downtown Havana where they lived to Bacuranao.

"Your house is too old and decrepit to be converted to a *casa particular,*" he told her. "But it's big enough to be traded in for a smaller, newer place on the beach."

Marlene didn't like hearing her late mother's home being called old and decrepit, but she reluctantly admitted that it had seen better days. The walls were peeling, and the electrical wiring had become a nightmare. The walls hadn't been painted in over thirty years. The tiles in the smoke-stained kitchen were beyond repair. The cast-iron stove, built in the early thirties, stood precariously on four bricks. A lot of money, which they didn't have, and skilled labor would be necessary to make the place livable again. And what use did they have for four rooms, anyway?

Yoel only contributed to the household budget when he sold a painting, which didn't happen often, and Marlene's salary as a National Revolutionary Police lieutenant wasn't enough to support both of them. His solution to generate some extra income was to set up a *casa particular* — a Cuban-style rental for foreigners — but clearly, their current home didn't meet the requirements.

"People who have beach houses want thousands of CUCs for them, not an old place in Centro Habana," Marlene told him.

"Not always," Yoel replied. "Papo, a friend of mine, knows a family that owns a duplex in Bacuranao. They are willing to trade half of it for a house."

"Even in the condition mine is now?"

"Yes, yes! They'll repair it. See, they rent part of the duplex to foreigners, forty CUCs a night, fifty or sixty in high season, and have saved enough cash to invest in a bigger place."

"Why do these folks want to get rid of a *casa particular* that's so profitable?" Marlene asked, suspicious.

"They need to split, *amor*. The parents are old and would rather live downtown, where they have better access to hospitals and other services. Their daughter and her kids will keep half of the duplex. It has two bedrooms, and one can still be rented. We'll do the same!"

In the end, Marlene agreed to the *permuta*. There were too many sad memories in her home. Her mother had died in the living room watching the eight o'clock news. In the dining room, Marlene had had a big fight with her brother before he left for Miami — she'd called him a despicable worm and a *cabrón*. Maybe it was better to begin a new life from scratch.

When Marlene said yes, Yoel hugged her and said, "We will be very happy there, my love."

He had been too exuberant, his eyes bright but averting hers. *I should have known,* Marlene chided herself. Why hadn't she noticed the red flags from the start? The detective instinct that had solved so many cases was deadened by the fragrance of Yoel's skin, kisses that tasted like chocolate and cream.

Yoel was the first man Marlene had wanted to marry. He claimed that he was ready too, but that there were problems, which he never fully explained. He and his wife had separated a long time ago, and their divorce was "almost final," he said. Marlene believed he had commitment issues, but would eventually come around. She was, after all, eight years his senior.

Georgina, Yoel's mother, hated her. Yoel was a graduate from the San Alejandro School of Art, and Georgina wanted another *artiste* for her son, not a cop. "A woman who carries a gun. Older than him. A *marimacha!*" Georgina's comments were reported to Marlene by an officious neighbor. They were hurtful, but she pretended not to care.

On the flip side, Yoel wasn't particularly popular among Marlene's friends. Her boss at Unidad 13, Captain Antonia Lujan, had met him at a party and hadn't been impressed.

"He isn't the right guy for you," she stated.

24

"Why do you say so?" Marlene asked.

"He doesn't have a job, for starters."

"He's an artist! He works for himself."

"Artist? A *comemierda,* that's what he is."

A shit-eater? Marlene didn't think so then.

"And there's something else about him," Antonia added. "He doesn't look people in the eye."

Marlene respected Antonia's judgement but in this case, she pushed it aside. Yes, she had noticed her partner's often furtive expression. He wasn't comfortable around cops, Yoel had confided, because he'd had a few brushes with the law. Nothing serious, just *maría,* as he called marijuana. Most artists used it, but he swore he didn't anymore.

After the *permuta* papers were signed, Yoel sold the entire contents of Marlene's house for one hundred dollars. The furniture was heavy and difficult to transport. "The collar will be more expensive than the dog if we try to move all of that to Bacuranao," he said when she argued for keeping some of the pieces. "And there isn't enough space in our half of the duplex."

It was painful to say goodbye to the armchair she always sat in to read the paper on Sunday morning, her mother's bed, the chest of drawers and the armoire that had been in the family since her grandparents'

25

wedding over seventy years ago, the full-sized mirror in front of which her grandma had fitted Marlene's *quinceañera* dress.

True, most pieces were damaged, unpainted and older than Marlene herself. The whole lot wasn't worth much. But how would they replace them? Yoel had it figured out: he'd give the money to a fine carpenter who would make new furniture for them: a sofa, a bed frame, a dining room table and chairs. "Everything built to our specifications," he said, giving her a long kiss.

Marlene never forgave herself for saying yes to that too. The moment she saw the mirror leave the house in the back of a truck, reflecting the street pavement on its clouded surface, she felt that some valuable, irreplaceable part of her life was being hauled away. But it was a done deal. Yoel pocketed the cash, which he promised to hand to the carpenter right away, and they moved to the Bacuranao duplex, or rather half duplex, the following day.

It didn't take long for Marlene to realize that Yoel was chummier with their neighbors, the family of three that stayed in the other part of the duplex, than he had originally let on. They were a middle-aged single mother and her children, a teenager named Luis and a pretty young woman,

Delia, who preferred bathing suits to regular clothes even for going to the grocery store.

Marlene wasn't the jealous type, but she couldn't help but notice that Delia was always hanging around the shared entrance of the building when Yoel came in or went out. Once she caught them talking. Not too close, and the conversation was innocent enough, something about surfboards and diving, but she made a mental note.

More worrisome was that Luis was the "fine carpenter" Yoel had entrusted with making their new furniture.

"The kid is barely old enough to be an apprentice!" Marlene said.

"He's very talented," Yoel answered. "He makes beautiful woodcarvings and sells them to tourists. He's an artist too."

Marlene wasn't convinced. "How long have you known these folks?"

"A couple of months," Yoel said, his eyes fixed on his own bare feet. "It was Papo who introduced us when I told him we were looking for a place on the beach, remember?"

Marlene had met some of his friends — other painters and a sculptor — but not Papo, who was preparing an exhibit in Holguín then, Yoel said. She made another mental note.

When they moved in to their new home, Luis was still working on the furniture, so they borrowed a motley assortment of pieces: a mattress on a metal frame, two chairs that didn't match, provided by Antonia, a smelly brown suede sofa, and a plastic table. They were all, Marlene realized with annoyance, much older and uglier than the ones she had owned.

There was no way they would be able to turn the place into a *casa particular* anytime soon. As days passed, Marlene made more mortifying discoveries: the toilet overflowed, the bedroom doors didn't lock, most of the metal fixtures were corroded by salt, and blackouts happened there more often than in Centro Habana. Within less than a month, her mental notes could have filled a phone book.

There was also the transportation problem. Marlene was still working at Unidad 13. Before, she used to walk to the station, but now she had to take three buses. She had petitioned to be transferred to a Bacuranao *unidad,* since there was a shortage of officers there, so there was hope this might be a temporary situation. But in the meantime, the twice-a-day trip could last hours. On Wednesdays, when she was on duty until 3 A.M., she spent the night with her aunt Isidra, who had an apartment on Espada Street, not far from Unidad 13. She didn't return home until Thursday evening.

It was a Wednesday when hell broke loose. The police station had been sprayed with a strong pesticide that made Marlene's allergies flare up. Noticing her watery eyes and runny nose, Antonia sent her home. She would cover for her that night. Marlene didn't have to report back until the following day at noon.

She sneezed all the way to her aunt's. But after taking a shower and resting for a while, she felt so much better that decided to go back to Bacuranao. Fresh air would do her good. Back in civilian clothes, she left her gun in Isidra's home, tucked under her uniform. She would swing by the next morning, change her clothes and retrieve it.

It wasn't like her to do that. Marlene seldom left her Makarov out of her sight, much less at the old lady's place. Now, her lips salty from the waves that crashed against the North Star, she realized that she subconsciously must have known what she would find at home.

She arrived in Bacuranao around four-thirty. She walked to the duplex, opened the door and entered the bedroom. The couple was naked on the borrowed mattress.

Her right hand went straight to her hip and found nothing.

"Thank God," Marlene said aloud as she watched the sun set. Her karate-trained arms and legs had done enough damage, but sending both Yoel and Delia to the hospital with multiple broken bones was different from sending them to the cemetery.

Marlene tried to return to the more pleasant reality of the cruise, angry for reliving the memory of an event from so long ago. It was these people's fault, Helen and Carlo-alberto. She hoped Emma would catch them.

4: PEER PRESSURE

They had been on the cruise for two days. Being away from land provided a sense of freedom that Marlene had never experienced before. She felt lighter, untethered. The fact that ordinary tasks like cooking and cleaning were taken care of by the crew made it even nicer. "This is a vacation from life," she told Sarita. The girl didn't seem to miss the high, dry desert where she lived or her parents. If only her best friends were there too, it would have been perfect, she said.

Marlene loved their stateroom, a cocoon of peace in the otherwise bustling onboard life. She didn't spend much time there, though. There was always something going on, from a musical to a hypnotism session (her favorite) to a short lecture about the sites they were visiting. Sarita was more inclined to head to the boutiques, the pool area and the game room, which had been designed specifically for teenagers since they couldn't gamble. Sarita was also usually magnetically drawn to whatever section of the ship Carloalberto happened to be in, which made Marlene nervous. The man seemed to attract trouble, and after yesterday, she suspected he deserved it.

Fortunately, they hadn't seen him in the past few hours. They had just come back from the pool, and Sarita was taking a shower. Marlene wanted to take one too, but knew from past experience that the girl wouldn't finish in less than fifteen minutes. She had just started singing, her words reverberating off the walls.

Having nothing more constructive to do, Marlene began to check her messages. She had left Max, a one-hundred-pound Rhodesian Ridgeback, with her cousin Candela. Max would be treated like a prince, but she still felt concerned. Aware of that, Candela had already sent a picture of him snoozing under a palm tree. Marlene smiled and texted her, *Gracias mil!* The dog had been her only companion since she'd moved to Miami three years ago.

Mercy Spivey, Marlene's business partner, was temporarily in charge of La Bakería Cubana. They had agreed that she would only contact her if there was an emergency.

Relieved to find nothing from Mercy, Marlene laid down on her bed, ready to relax. Her initial concerns about something going wrong in the cruise began to fade. It would just be a fun, aunt-niece bonding kind of trip.

A minute later, she heard a ping on Sarita's phone — the girl had left it on Marlene's bed, so she glanced distractedly at the incoming WhatsApp message in a group chat named "Carloalberto Fans."

Jane: Did u do it?

Do what? Intrigued, Marlene unlocked the phone, hitting "2" several times, and read on.

Lupe: Yeah, r u done?

Jane and Lupe — weren't these the girls who had gotten Sarita into trouble? They were supposedly reformed, but you never knew with kids. Just in case, Marlene scrolled up to the beginning of the chat.

Sarita: Still trying
Jane: Can't b 2 hard
Sarita: It is with M around all day
Jane: Hurry up. We have 2 finish this!
Sarita: Gimme some time, bitches

Marlene winced. Not only did she not approve of teenage girls calling each other "bitches," but Sarita's friends were trying to get her to do something that probably had to do with Carloalberto. Something Marlene, or M, wasn't supposed to know.

The sound of water in the shower stopped, but Sarita was still singing her heart out. Marlene inspected her call log. She had made two the first day of the trip, July 12, to different area code 575 numbers. Jane and Lupe? She remembered Sarita's excitement on the phone. She must have called her friends right after discovering that Carloalberto was on board. Marlene checked the WhatsApp group again. It had also been created on July 12.

She left the phone on the bed and walked to the balcony. Sarita came out of the bathroom, toweling her hair. She looked older than her fifteen years, with "Caribbean" curves and a fresh, rosy face that didn't need the fake eyelashes and red lipstick she chose to wear. She had inherited her father's dark hair and her mother's blue eyes. She was already turning into a beauty, often attracting men's stares.

Marlene fought the urge to ask her about the WhatsApp group. Looking at somebody's messages was probably a criminal offense in Sarita's world, akin to reading private diary entries in Marlene's generation. It could ruin the whole trip. Besides, it would be easier to watch her niece if she didn't suspect anything. Maybe all her friends wanted was a picture of Carloalberto or a selfie of him and Sarita.

Or not. Marlene remembered her sister-in-law cautioning her to "keep the girl on a short leash." Sarita had been in trouble largely due to peer pressure, her father had said. Because of these two girls. When Sarita announced she was going to browse the boutiques, Marlene insisted on accompanying her.

Later that evening, they ate again at The Ambassador. Without Carloalberto there, Sarita admitted that she didn't really enjoy the place; it was too formal for her taste and didn't allow shorts or sandals. But Marlene insisted. The desserts alone were worth donning a pair of nice shoes.

Per usual, the girl tried to start a conversation about Carloalberto's good looks, but Marlene redirected the conversation to a couple of the cases she'd solved back in Cuba. Sarita listened attentively, more interested than she would ever admit.

"Did you like being a cop, Tía?" she asked over her spaghetti Bolognese.

"I did," Marlene answered. "It wasn't always easy, and political issues made it tougher, but I enjoyed my work."

"Was it dangerous?"

"Sometimes."

Sarita cocked her head slightly to one side, then whispered, "Did you carry a gun every day?"

"Every day I was on duty, yes," Marlene said, flashing back to the Bacuranao incident, which she had no intention of sharing.

"What kind was it?"

"An old Russian model. You've probably never heard of it."

"Do you own one now?"

"Goodness, no, *mijita*. What for?"

"Could you teach me how to shoot?"

"Not in a million years," Marlene laughed.

A man wearing a chef's hat and an immaculate white apron walked by their table and glanced at them, but Marlene barely noticed.

The main course finished, the waiter brought out the guava caramel bread pudding — large enough to share — that Marlene had chosen for dessert, intrigued by the guava addition. At the sight of the candied pecans layered over the pudding, Sarita whistled. They dove right in, munch-

36

ing ecstatically for a few minutes.

"Would you ever become a cop again in Miami?" the girl asked after the bowl was completely clean.

"I don't think so. My English isn't good enough, for one thing. Besides," Marlene licked her lips, "being a baker is more fun."

"But not as cool as being a detective."

Marlene laughed. "I'm past the cool stage, *mijita*. What about you? Any idea of what you want to do when you grow up?"

"I'd like to be a journalist," Sarita said thoughtfully. "It's cool, fun, even a little dangerous."

"Every job that involves finding out the truth has an element of danger," Marlene agreed.

Sarita nodded.

"I'm not scared of danger," she announced.

Marlene sighed. "I know. But I'm scared for you, *mijita*."

5: THE SHAMANA'S PROPHECY

The bus was headed to the Stann Creek district of Belize, where a local *shamana* would give them a talk about jungle plants and Mayan ceremonies. The tour guide was a short, muscular young man named Manuel who spoke fluent English, Spanish and Maya. "You guys are lucky; you're going to meet the most famous female healer in Stann Creek," he told the group. "We had to schedule this eight months in advance — she's that in demand!"

Marlene had booked the excursion out of curiosity, wondering how different shamans were from Santería practitioners. She wasn't a believer, but one of her best friends in Cuba was a highly respected *santero.* She was hoping to write him a letter — a *real* one, handwritten and stamped — about her findings. Though she used email for work, Marlene wasn't a big fan of the Internet.

Sarita hadn't been interested in meeting

the *shamana* at first, but changed her mind when she discovered that Carloalberto, Helen and Emma had signed up for the excursion too. When they got on the small, air-conditioned bus, Sarita positioned herself behind Emma, who had a window seat, and Carloalberto. Helen was on the aisle seat across from him. Marlene sat next to her niece and watched the couple's exchanges, which looked quite ordinary:

"More water, *mi amor*?" Carloalberto asked Emma, offering her a plastic bottle.

"Not right now, *papi,* but keep it handy. We'll need to stay hydrated."

Their interaction was far more cordial than at the icy dinner the other night. Maybe Carloalberto had acted fast enough on the balcony that his wife didn't suspect his fling. Maybe it didn't even occur to her to consider the screenwriter a romantic rival, or maybe she just didn't care.

Carloalberto checked his cell phone every five minutes and complained about the poor Internet connection. Emma listened to Manuel, looking bored with his stories.

"She always looks like someone has farted in her face," Sarita muttered.

As for Helen, she seemed to be having problems with her smartphone. She kept touching the screen and cursing under her breath.

"It's not just the Internet, I can't even access my voicemail," she said, exasperated.

"Smartphones are stupid," Emma deigned to say. "What's worse, they make people stupid. I barely use mine. I check my email only once a week, if that."

Marlene had the impression that Emma had called the screenwriter "stupid" in a not-so-veiled way.

"It's like the devil himself is messing with me," Helen muttered, ignoring the comment.

"Now, let's not bring *el diablo* up," Manuel said with a smile. "He might decide to pay us a visit."

"I hope not. But I'd gladly throw this damn thing at him!"

Finally, Carloalberto helped Helen figure out how to take pictures with her phone. She started snapping away.

"Not to sound like a *dinosaur,* but I prefer plain old cameras," Helen said, looking critically at the shots. "Just like I prefer to write my scripts by hand. I only use a computer to type up the final version."

Carloalberto chuckled.

"Wow, she *is* a dinosaur," Sarita whispered to her aunt.

"Well, so am I," Marlene replied. Despite herself, she was starting to feel sympathetic for Helen.

The road led to the Cockscomb Basin Wildlife Sanctuary, the only jaguar preserve in the world. A few tourists craned their necks outside, hoping to get a glimpse of a wandering jaguar, although Manuel had already told them it was extremely rare to see one in daylight.

To keep them entertained during the two-hour trip, he told them about the Mayan civilization that had inhabited the area long before the arrival of the Spanish *conquistadores:* their use of obsidian tools, their ball games and elaborate calendar.

"So what happened to them?" a tourist asked. "Why did they disappear?"

"They didn't disappear," the guide replied. "Look at me! I am Mayan. My wife and I speak Mayan at home. The *shamana* we are going to meet and her family are all Mayan. Although many of the original inhabitants of this region up and left, possibly because of a drought, others stayed and mixed with Olmecs and Toltecs, and later with the Spaniards. We are still here, but hidden in plain sight."

Carloalberto was taking pictures of the

landscape, Manuel, other passengers and a few selfies for good measure. Emma rolled her eyes but said nothing. Except for Sarita, who looked enthralled, no one else on the bus appeared to recognize him or his companions.

"Are you sure you and your friends aren't the only ones who watch that *Terrific*-whatever program?" Marlene whispered to her niece.

"Of course not! It's super popular!" the girl replied, offended.

"If you say so."

"This bus is just full of people who live under a rock."

The *shamana*'s domain was a compound built around a big *palapa* structure. A brick house and five straw huts were scattered nearby. There were mango and orange trees, flowering shrubs and blooming orchids everywhere. It smelled of damp earth and smoke.

Someone was cooking on a wood stove outside the *palapa*. Marlene sniffed the air. Yes, it was the unmistakable aroma of rice being boiled in coconut oil. The visit included lunch, and her stomach growled in anticipation. She was getting tired of the cruise menu. No matter how good the chefs were, food made for thousands of people

43

always tasted mass-produced because, well, it was. Except for the desserts at The Ambassador, which seemed to be in a class of their own.

The group was led to the *palapa,* where they sat on red, blue and yellow cushions on the floor. The *shamana,* a short woman with jet-black hair and intense obsidian eyes, brought them snacks: Mayan-style chocolate mixed with cornmeal, ripe mangoes and round pastries drizzled with honey.

Her talk revolved around green medicine and herbal remedies.

"The *cocolmeca* or male *dioscorea* has a Viagra-like effect," she said with a wink. "Boil it in water and take three cups per day. The results are miraculous!"

Some took notes, either using their smartphones or on old-fashioned pieces of paper. Carloalberto asked the *shamana* if he could record her talk on his phone. The *shamana* agreed, joking she should charge him extra for it. When she got ready to take the party for a walk of her botanical garden, Helen asked, "Aren't we going to do a ceremony first?"

"Yeah!" Carloalberto said, enthusiastically. "Something for good luck, like a *limpia.*"

Emma rolled her eyes again.

"I could do a *tzite* seeds reading," the *sha-*

mana answered. "The *tzite* is one of our most sacred trees. It's not for good luck, but more of a prediction tool."

"That'll be fine too."

"Bear in mind that I tell it as I see it. Sometimes people get bad news and yell at me. This isn't 'for entertainment only,' as clairvoyants do in your country. Here, you have to be willing to hear the truth."

"How much will that be?" Helen asked.

"Twenty dollars per person," the *shamana* replied. "Readings aren't included in the regular tour."

"Fair enough."

The botanical garden walk was forgotten as people got in line for their readings.

"What a waste of time and money," Marlene complained, but she got in line as well.

The readings were fast. A quick-and-dirty consultation, Marlene ascertained. Most of her fellow passengers were beaming when they came out of the straw hut where the *shamana* had set up shop.

"It's like she knew me my whole life!"

"Remarkable. It was all true."

Americans were so naïve. Marlene smirked, now completely convinced that the woman was a con artist. How come no one had received the promised bad news? But she couldn't avoid feeling apprehensive

45

when her turn came and she sat down in front of the *shamana*. Between them was a red and white rug that smelled strongly of copal.

The *shamana* opened a blue cloth bag — "my sacred bundle," she called it — took out a bunch of bright red seeds, blew on them, prayed silently and spread them over the dirt floor. That reminded Marlene of her friend Padrino, the *santero*. Sometimes he was right, she conceded. Bah, probably by chance.

"Your life's about to change," the *shamana* said.

Marlene waited, unimpressed by the platitude. Wasn't everyone's life constantly changing?

"You used to make a living following blood trails, and you'll do it once more," the *shamana* went on. "You are a natural-born bloodhound and will soon follow another trail."

Marlene was too shocked to say a word. She handed the *shamana* twenty dollars and hurried out, the smell of copal lingering in her nose. She wanted to stop Sarita from going in, but it was too late; the girl had pranced into the hut within seconds.

"I'm going to fulfill a dream of mine, but in a way that's totally unexpected," she

46

reported five minutes later. "Maybe it's about me becoming a journalist?"

"Hmm, it's possible," Marlene said. "Did she say anything about that Carloalberto guy? I bet you asked about him!"

Sarita's ears burned hot. "It looked like my news *may* have something to do with him. Now, would you please give me a twenty so I can pay this lady?"

"Fine," said Marlene, pulling the bill from her wallet. "But I want to hear more about it later."

She couldn't believe she was so concerned about the *shamana*'s predictions. Of course these things were just local lore! But the accuracy of the woman's earlier words had unsettled her.

When the readings were over, Manuel called the tourists to the *palapa,* where dishes piled high with steaming rice and vegetables awaited them. Marlene took her time to join the group. She noticed that Sarita had managed to sit next to Carloalberto. Shaking her head, she walked toward the *palapa,* but her hunger had vanished.

6: The Pastry Chef

It was well past two when Marlene woke up on the lounge chair where she had been taking a nap. Sarita was in the Jacuzzi, talking to another girl and, her aunt noticed with a mix of astonishment and annoyance, taking selfies. It was their final day in Belize. In the early morning, they had gone for a short visit to a nearby bird sanctuary, returned at ten-thirty, before it got too hot, and hung out in the pool area until Marlene found a cool spot under a big blue umbrella and fell asleep.

Sarita wasn't hungry. She had been snacking at the Forest Café since they came back. But Marlene was starving. She took a shower and changed into her new yellow tunic dress that made her look younger and carefree. A pair of amber earrings she had brought would have complemented it nicely, but she didn't wear them. She wasn't trying to impress anybody, after all.

She went down to The Ambassador alone and ordered fried ravioli and eggplant parmigiana. For dessert, the waiter suggested a slice of bonbon cake.

"It's our pastry chef's signature dish," he said.

"I'll take it!"

The cake had a thin layer of solid chocolate on top, strawberry- and almond-flavored meringue inside, and truffles all around. Tiny pieces of chopped almond and chocolate chips added texture to the icing. It was served cold with two scoops of pistachio ice cream. Marlene nearly swooned when she had the first bite. She was always looking for inspiration and new items to add to La Bakería Cubana's offerings. Like the guava bread pudding, this one was a keeper. She savored it slowly, having trained her palate to identify the flavors in order to reproduce them. There was a hint of vanilla. Nutmeg, perhaps? Definitely a bit of Kahlua.

It would be perfect for a wedding cake, she mused. A week ago, she had made a coconut cake crowned with meringue-covered figurines. In a bonbon cake, the groom's suit and tie would be dark chocolate. The bride's dress, whipped cream frosting —

Her dreamy expression prompted the waiter to ask how she had liked it, and her enthusiastic response brought the pastry chef to her table. He was of medium height, with fine features and an olive complexion. They started chatting in English, but soon found out both were native Spanish speakers and changed linguistic gears.

Benito, the pastry chef, was from Oaxaca, Mexico. "Like Benito Juárez," he remarked with a smile and a twist of his dark eyebrows.

"Your cake," Marlene said, "has no mother."

She had learned this expression from her Mexican friends. To say that something had no mother, or no grandmother, meant that it was terrific. It could be used to mean the opposite too, but it was clear that wasn't the case here.

"Thanks!"

After some small talk, Benito, who had finished his shift, invited her to walk around the promenade deck. They had just departed from Belize. It had cooled down, and the breeze off the ocean was refreshing.

Marlene asked him about the crew's daily life. She had thought of joining an onboard security team in the unlikely event that she got tired of the bakery. Benito seemed to enjoy answering her many questions.

"I'm on a three-month contract, so I have no days off for twelve weeks," he said. "After five or six trips, it becomes a rotation of faces going around to the same places. But *some* faces," he raised his eyebrows at Marlene, "stand out. I noticed you the first day you came to The Ambassador."

She briefly regretted not having worn her amber earrings, but swatted the thought away. She'd never been a flirt, and he was just trying to flatter her. No way he would have noticed her with so many younger, more attractive women around.

She stopped herself. *Now I'm the one thinking like an insecure teenager.*

"I imagine it never gets old," she said.

"It does, believe me. There comes a time when you can finish the passengers' sentences and even predict when a fight's going to happen. Not that we have too many, of course."

"Is security here tight? I've heard passengers are on camera more often than they'd suspect."

"Except for the staterooms, most areas are monitored, yes. There are always shenanigans going on. We just need to make sure they don't get out of hand."

Shenanigans, huh?

"Do you like working here?" Marlene asked.

"It's been good, despite the crazy hours. I don't have to commute, do laundry or pay rent while I'm on board. But I'm only planning to be here until the end of the year, then quit and work in a restaurant or patisserie to see another side of the business before I open my own place. It's a dream I have had for a long time." He leaned against the railing and grinned, "Well, enough about me. What about you? What do you do?"

Marlene smiled knowingly. "I had the same dream once. Made it a reality two years ago in Miami. It's called La Bakería Cubana."

"But a *vaquería* is a dairy!"

They laughed.

"Just a bit of Spanglish wordplay. Most people don't even catch it," Marlene said.

"Are you Puerto Rican?"

"Cuban. But you have a good ear. Our accents are very close, just like our flags."

"Oh, Cuban!" He looked surprised. "*Órale.* Have you always been a baker?"

"Not really. I used to be a detective in Havana."

"A detective . . . for Castro?"

"For the police force, making sure people

53

were safe." Marlene hoped politics wouldn't ruin the conversation. Her brother had advised her to say she used to work in a *paladar,* a Cuban private restaurant, but she hated lying. She was relieved when Benito said, "Of course, I'm sorry. That was silly of me to say."

Goodness, a man who could apologize! It ticked a few notches in his favor. "Don't worry, I get it all the time. And worse."

"What brought you to Miami, Marlene?"

The answer was long and too complicated for a new acquaintance. It involved her slow, painful disillusion with the system, wanting to mend her relationship with her brother, who had left Cuba on a raft in the nineties and, though she would never admit it to herself, the way things with Yoel had ended. But she only said, "Family matters and wanting to start my own business."

He laughed. "The only family I have is a Chihuahua. How about you? Married with children?"

Marlene smiled. "No, neither. But I have a dog too, a Rhodesian Ridgeback"

"I thought the girl you've been with this entire time was your daughter," Benito said.

So he'd noticed them earlier.

"She's my niece."

The North Star was on the open sea now.

There was no trace of land in any direction, as if the ship was suspended between ocean and sky.

"You know," Benito said, "That bonbon cake you liked so much, I've been perfecting it for years. One day, I'll serve it to guests at my wedding."

7: A TRAGEDY

Marlene was waiting for Sarita on the promenade deck. It had become her favorite place after that walk with Benito. There, she could look at the ocean and enjoy the fresh air away from the noisy crowd congregated around the swimming pools and Jacuzzis on deck fifteen. Sometimes she smoked a cigarette, feeling both smug for getting away with it and ashamed for being unable to quit.

They were still sailing. There wasn't much to do on board that evening, only a Spanish-language lesson in the library, which neither Marlene nor Sarita needed, and a bingo game that had made them yawn after the first five minutes. The casino and all the boutiques were open, but Marlene was neither a gambler nor a compulsive shopper. Even Sarita was tired of seeing the same overpriced stuff.

Marlene had been thinking back to her

meeting with the *shamana*. She wondered if there was some signal she'd given the woman that she'd once been a "bloodhound." And the prophecy that she would be one again? She doubted it. There were too many reasons to never go back to that line of work in Miami, her limited English and longing for a quiet life among them. It was why she had opened La Bakería Cubana, which had become popular among the new wave of Cubans looking for *mazarreales* — thick guava pastries, as opposed to the traditional puffy ones — croquettes and yuca fries.

The trip had been good inspiration for the bakery. Being away from the oven was giving Marlene the time she needed to think up new recipes. Right now, she was concocting a pastry filled with Mayan-style chocolate, sprinkled with coconut flakes, perfect for the mild Miami winters. She would run it by Benito. And ask him about that bonbon cake . . .

Her reveries were cut short when Sarita appeared, sobbing.

"Ay, Tía! What a tragedy!"

"What is it?" asked Marlene, startled. "What happened?"

"Carloalberto!" the girl sniffled. "He's been eliminated."

A shudder ran through Marlene. "What do you mean?"

"From the show. He and Helen were finalists, and everybody expected them to win, but the vote was today, and they got the boot. The hosts seemed disappointed and said Carloalberto had a future in the film industry, but still —"

Marlene let out a sigh. "That's what you call a tragedy, *mijita*?"

"For me it is! For all his fans. He must be devastated. Would it be wrong to go up to him and offer my condolences?"

"Very," Marlene said firmly. "How did you even watch this, anyway? I thought we didn't get cable here."

Sarita waved her smartphone.

"Come on, Tía! This is the twenty-first century! My friends are following the show and have been texting me the whole time. It's on Facebook, too."

Ah, social media. It had replaced personal interaction, seeming to rule lives. Someday, Marlene thought, it would rule their deaths, too. People would die in front of their smartphones, breathing their last into the screen.

"I read that Carloalberto has some pretty bad gambling debts," Sarita added with a concerned expression. "I hope he'll be okay."

Marlene remembered the man in the Hawaiian shirt and his not-so-veiled threats.

"We all have our vices," she said stoically.

"Like your cigarettes, eh?" Sarita said.

Marlene winced. "Hey, I —"

"Here they come!"

Carloalberto and Emma were on the promenade deck walking toward them. He had his arms wrapped around her, and they were smiling at each other. Marlene shook her head. Men.

"He doesn't look upset at all," she said. "Tell me, how could the show run tonight without him even present?"

"Their segments were submitted in advance," Sarita explained. "Carloalberto and Helen already filmed several scenes of the movie they're hoping to produce. He plays a king."

"A king?" Marlene made a funny face. "What kind of movie is this?"

"Historical. I mean, historical plus fantasy. Like King Arthur meets *Game of Thrones*."

"*Alabao!*"

"Don't '*alabao*' me! This is serious, Tía. Their clips were so good, and now they're out of the running. How sad! They were so close."

"Yes, sad indeed," Marlene said, feeling no sadness at all. "Now, come walk with me."

Before they completed a lap around the promenade deck, Benito caught up with them. He was in a hurry and wearing his chef hat.

"Just to tell you, my dessert tonight is inspired by you," he said to Marlene, just quietly enough that Sarita couldn't hear. "It's called Havana Nights. Cinnamon, meringue and a sip of rum."

Marlene fought back a blush. "Sounds good! I'll try it."

"Who was that guy?" Sarita asked with a raised eyebrow after Benito left.

"The pastry chef at The Ambassador," Marlene answered, feigning indifference.

The girl wasn't so easily fooled. *"Ese huevo quiere sal,"* she said. "Which *doesn't* mean an egg wants salt, but that someone wants —"

"Shh, *mijita*! You're getting too smart for your own good," Marlene said, laughing.

Around eight o'clock, Sarita went to a jewelry sale on deck six, and Marlene returned to their stateroom to properly dress for dinner. She didn't want to show up at The Ambassador wearing the same yellow tunic this time.

61

Her door was open. A vacuum cleaner stood in the hall next to a big trash bag. The cleaning crew was tidying the cabins, which usually didn't take more than ten minutes, but the lack of security worried Marlene. Anyone could waltz in and take other passengers' valuables. She would mention it to Benito.

Faced with her own minimal wardrobe, Marlene peeked over at Sarita's and picked out a dress. It was long and flowing, not overly young. Fortunately, they had similar body types. Unlike her niece, Marlene was proud of her ample behind. She looked in the mirror and smiled at her reflection, then said aloud that she wasn't interested in impressing anyone.

Back in the hall, she ran into Helen, whose cabin was two doors away. The screenwriter was sobbing.

She's the only one who looks devastated.

That contest must have meant more to her than it had to Carloalberto. Helen wasn't so young. Carloalberto was just starting his career, but she might be nearing the end of hers.

8: Phone Overboard

The North Star would dock in the Costa Maya port sometime before midnight. At seven o'clock on a packed deck fifteen, tanned and slightly drunk passengers danced to "La Bamba." Others sipped mojitos or soaked in the hot tubs. The wind was balmy, and the sun set in a burst of copper hues. The sky stretched in a perfect arc above the ship.

"Selfie time!" Sarita announced, posing in front of her phone.

Other passengers all seemed to have the same idea. Carloalberto, in the company of "his women," as Marlene had come to think of them, snapped pictures of himself and his companions near the mojito bar. Emma was her usual bored, indifferent self, while Helen seemed to have recovered from the "tragedy" of being knocked out of the contest, laughing and posing with her friends.

The image of Yoel returned to pester Marlene. Come to think of it, he and Carloalberto could have been brothers. Both were tall and dark-haired and possessed the kind of swagger that had at first attracted her. It also struck her that her relationship with Yoel had been similar to Helen's with Carloalberto, though of course she hadn't known it at the time. It wasn't until several months after the Bacuranao incident that she'd found out the truth: Yoel's divorce had never been "almost final." He was very much married to an older Spanish woman who'd finally gotten him a visa to join her in Madrid. Marlene had just been someone he'd felt he could profit off in the meantime.

She spat on the waves and glowered at Carloalberto. He was looking nervous now, and she knew why: just a few feet away from them stood the blond man who'd threatened him the first day of the trip. He kept an obvious eye on the aspiring actor, who had a forced smile plastered on his Botoxed face.

The stories Sarita had read about Carloalberto's gambling debts were likely true. He spent hours at a time in the casino. But so did the other passengers, especially when there was nothing more exciting on the schedule. It didn't matter — Marlene didn't feel much sympathy for him.

"Ouch!" Sarita yelped.

She had stumbled on the wet floor and lost her balance trying to hold herself and her phone at the same time. Marlene hurried to steady her. "You're going to end up breaking a bone with all this selfie garbage!"

"It would be worse if I broke the phone," Sarita replied.

Carloalberto asked Helen to take a selfie of the usual threesome. They put their heads together and the screenwriter fumbled with her phone, finally flipping its perspective to the front camera. "Say cheese!" she yelled.

Sinvergüenza, Marlene thought, glaring at Carloalberto. The guy didn't have an ounce of shame. Neither did Helen. Marlene looked away, disgusted, and scanned the crowd for Benito, who had promised to join her when he finished his shift, and didn't see what happened next. But she, along with everyone else on deck, heard Helen's cry. "My phone!"

A small crowd congregated around her, looking at the water where the device had disappeared after slipping from her hand.

"You dropped it?"

"Yeah."

"So sorry!"

"Oh, it's fine. Never got along very well

with that thing," the screenwriter said with a sigh.

Sarita was horrified. Marlene laughed.

"See what happens when you go around taking selfies like an *estúpida?*" she told her niece.

Her words fell on deaf ears. As Sarita took rapid-fire shots of Helen, Carloalberto and the rest of the commiserating pack, Marlene realized what the girl's WhatsApp messages had been about. Sarita's friends must have asked her for close-ups of Carloalberto, Emma and Helen. They probably had an entire gallery in "the cloud" devoted to that *comemierda.*

"Poor Helen," Sarita said later, holding her phone carefully. "First she loses the contest, now her phone — nothing worse than not having your phone. She should have asked for a *limpia* from the Belize witch."

"The *shamana* wasn't offering *limpias,*" Marlene reminded her. "But Helen can get one in Costa Maya tomorrow."

Once the ruckus was over, Marlene petitioned Sarita to accompany her to the library.

"It's the only place on the ship you haven't been yet," she said. "Reading is important!"

Marlene had never been an avid reader

herself, but the library happened to be on the same deck as The Ambassador.

"I know that," Sarita said. "I have all the books I need in my Kindle." But she followed her aunt anyway.

The library was a small room with barely enough space for a leather sofa, three armchairs, a table covered with games — chess, Monopoly and checkers — and two bookshelves that featured travel guides, paperback mysteries and romance novels. An electric fireplace with fake logs in the corner looked somewhat out of place.

Sarita sniggered at the board games and leafed through a couple of books, but none of them held her attention for long. Apart from an older couple playing Scrabble, the room was deserted.

"There's nothing here," the girl pronounced.

The loudspeakers informed passengers that the raffle had started in one of the boutiques. Of course Sarita begged to go, even though Marlene warned her that this was likely just an ordinary sale in disguise of the items that had been languishing on the shelves since the beginning of the trip.

Then Sarita, who had been checking her phone, exclaimed, "Oh my god, Tía! Look at this."

She showed Marlene an online article from *The Miami Herald.*

"Despite being voted off *The Terrific Two,* the young Cuban actor is being eyed for the lead role in a new film," the girl read, emotion choking her words. "Dubbed the next William Levy, Carloalberto says his agent is in talks with several producers about future roles."

"What about Helen?" Marlene asked. "It doesn't seem like she's been offered anything."

"On the show, they talk about how screenwriters who aren't established by that age have an even harder time finding work than actors," Sarita said. "She's probably out of luck. But hopefully *we* aren't, so let's go buy raffle tickets! And don't forget the party tonight at the Icelandic Bar." She ran toward the elevators.

"Wait!" Marlene shouted after her. "You can't just walk into a bar, you know that."

"The party is eighteen and under! Check the schedule if you don't believe me."

"Okay, we'll see."

Benito came out of The Ambassador and walked over to Marlene. "*Hola*! I was just thinking about you. Are you coming to the restaurant to eat?"

"Not yet," Marlene said, smiling. "I just

wanted to bring my niece to the library. She *loves* to read."

9: The Night of "El Rey"

The party was indeed family-friendly. Why the heck had they chosen to throw it at one of the ship's bars, of all places? Marlene would have rather attended another Blue Man show, but there was no stopping Sarita. She had won nothing at the raffle but didn't care: she was now fixated on the strobe-lit dance floor.

The girl stood in front of the mirror, applying cherry-red lipstick as if her future depended on perfectly drawn outlines. She wore a tight black dress with a revealing neckline, high heels and way too much blush. Marlene didn't approve of the outfit, but Sarita swore that her own mother had bought the dress for her.

"Could you please stop acting like an uptight spinster?" she complained. "You used to be fun!"

"Yes, and you used to behave," Marlene replied.

"I *am* behaving!"

"Like a *guanaja.*"

"A goose?"

"Maybe worse."

The fact that Benito was still on shift at The Ambassador — one of the cooks had called in sick — probably accounted for Marlene's foul mood. The last thing she wanted to do was attend a party.

"By the way," Sarita turned around and blotted her lips with a tissue, "Carloalberto's on the passenger list for the 'swimming with dolphins' excursion tomorrow. Can we go too? Please?"

Marlene had planned to visit the Tulum ruins the following day, but the temperature was expected to hit the high nineties. She had already been reconsidering, and Sarita knew it.

"We don't need to see *two* ruins, Tía," she pleaded. "We're going to Chichen Itza on Friday, and all those sites look the same. There's never a place to pee in any of them, and they're so hot and boring. I'm sick and tired of that Mayan stuff!"

Marlene was getting pretty sick and tired of Sarita's sass, but reminded herself that this trip was a gift to her niece. So what if all she wanted out of it was to be around a semi-famous actor? It was all harmless.

Thankfully, Carloalberto hadn't given a single sign that he'd noticed her. Too much on his plate to acknowledge a teenage fangirl. Marlene hoped he would stay busy with "his women" and that loan shark until they returned to Miami. In the end, she relented and called reception to book the excursion. It would be cooler than Tulum, shorter, cheaper. And she liked dolphins too.

"Thank you, Tía!" Sarita hugged her. "This means a lot to me. I can't believe I'll get to be in a swimming pool with Carloalberto!"

"You and two dozen other people," Marlene muttered.

"So?" Sarita shrugged and turned back to the mirror. "At least Emma isn't going. I didn't see her on the list. She probably doesn't want to get sunburned. And Helen's no competition."

"I'm sorry, competition for what?" Marlene asked sternly.

Sarita blushed and shook her head. "I mean — never mind."

"Competition for *what*?"

"Oh — you know, Tía. I just want to talk to Carloalberto."

This was the problem, Marlene realized. The girl was so young, she was confusing a celebrity crush for an ordinary one — she'd

73

never had a boyfriend and had been painfully shy until just a couple years ago.

"Talk about what, *por Dios*?"

"So many things. Like his career."

"What career, *mija*? How many movies has he been in?"

Sarita pursed her bright-red lips in thought.

"A few. Short ones, but still. Some really cool commercials, and two telenovelas — he was a gang member in one and a lawyer in the other. There are others if you count bit roles. And obviously *The Terrific Two.* Plus that new movie they're talking about!" She swallowed and said in a low voice, "If it goes well, I might even ask him out."

Marlene had no words for her niece, knowing this silly, innocent teenage crush had only become alarming in the vicinity of Carloalberto. But what was normal for a Cuban American teenager, anyway? Marlene was happy she didn't have any of her own to worry about, but she was responsible for Sarita, at least for the duration of the cruise. All she could do was keep a careful eye on her.

The party started around 8:30 P.M. The Icelandic Bar overflowed with underwhelming free canapés, overpriced cocktails and a discordant band. There were throbbing lights, a disco ball and smoke coming from a fog machine, which disoriented some people to the point that they were stepping on others' feet. By ten o'clock, most of the attendees were too drunk to walk around without bumping into their fellow passengers.

The band was playing old ballads. Some people belted out, in a pitiful Mexican accent, the last verses of "El Rey." Sarita's eyes teared up as she sang about the man who, with or without money, always did what he wanted. The misunderstood guy who had no throne or queen, but was still king.

"Where do you think my king is?" the girl asked when she couldn't find Carloalberto.

"Probably off gambling."

Despite the thrill of being inside a real bar for the first time, it was a night of disappointment for Sarita. An hour later, Carloalberto still hadn't shown. Neither had "his women," for that matter.

"I can't believe it," Sarita sighed, slumping into a chair and taking her heels off. "How could he not show up?"

Marlene was about to try to comfort her niece when the girl popped up, still barefoot, and headed straight to the casino. Marlene had no choice but to follow. Carloalberto was at the roulette table, fear and desperation on his face.

"I guess he does have a gambling problem," Sarita sighed. "I wish I could help him."

"Good grief."

"Maybe I can go talk to him?"

Marlene narrowed her eyes. "Not unless you want this to be the last cruise you ever take with me."

"Oh, Tía."

"Come on, let's go back to that idiotic shindig."

Helen and Emma had shown up at the party. The screenwriter immediately became a withering wallflower, though a very thirsty wallflower, Marlene noticed. She'd downed three margaritas and a shot of tequila in less than half an hour. Not happy with that, she flagged a waiter down. "A gin martini," she said, slurring her words.

Oh boy, thought Marlene.

Emma danced with the blond guy in the Hawaiian shirt. Marlene overheard her call him "Fernando" in a familiar tone, but their interactions seemed more businesslike than romantic. They looked more intent on talking than dancing and hardly moved around the room.

Helen disappeared around ten-thirty, and Emma and Fernando left half an hour later. Though Marlene wanted to go outside for a while, she didn't dare leave her niece alone. But when the band began to play "El Rey" for the third time, she'd had enough. The blaring music was giving her a headache, all the food was gone and Sarita was talking to a couple of girls her age, so Marlene sneaked out to the deck and lit up a cigarette. Another middle-aged woman was out here too. They exchanged guilty smiles and went about their business.

It was a good spot. No one else was around, and the party noises were barely audible. The waves were dark and gentle, and stars shone through thin clouds. Why would anyone in their right mind be inside a closed room instead of enjoying the beauty of the ocean at night? Marlene inhaled the smoke and started to feel better. She wished Benito were there too.

Her cigarette was almost finished when a loud splash made her jump.

"What was that?" her companion asked.

"I don't know, but it sounded heavy," Marlene replied.

Like a body being thrown overboard.

She rushed back to the Icelandic Bar and looked for Sarita, but the girl was nowhere to be found. Marlene went down to the casino and ran to the roulette table. Carlo-alberto had vanished, too. She remembered the WhatsApp messages.

Did u do it? R u done?

What if the girl's friends had wanted something more than pictures? Something that had put Sarita's safety at risk?

10: A DAY IN COSTA MAYA

The next morning, the passengers who had signed up for the "swimming with dolphins" trip gathered on land to wait for their guide. Helen was ready, sporting a big Panama hat, but Carloalberto hadn't joined them yet.

Sarita was crestfallen. Marlene had read her the riot act the previous night. It had taken her forty-five minutes to find the girl on deck fifteen, hanging out near the pools. Sarita claimed she had gone there with her "new besties" because they'd gotten bored at the party, but Marlene detected alcohol on her niece's breath. No doubt the girls had found someone unscrupulous enough to buy drinks for a bunch of teenage girls.

"You pull that on me again, we're leaving this cruise immediately. And your parents will definitely hear all about it," Marlene had threatened.

Now, head low, Sarita didn't even dare to look at her.

At eight-thirty, Adriana, a young and energetic Mexican guide, arrived and greeted the group.

"Welcome to Mahahual!" she said. "Our dolphin's name is Plato. He's very sweet and loves to meet new people. And he's bilingual, too! Let's go see him."

"Could we wait a minute?" Helen asked. "We're still missing someone."

"Sorry, *señora,*" Adriana answered. "We have a specific time slot reserved in the pool. If we're late, we'll lose it."

"But my friend was so looking forward to this! And it's already paid for."

The people around them started to complain.

"You friend could still be sleeping, for all we know," another passenger said to Helen. "Why don't you just call him?"

"I lost my phone!"

"He can meet us at the pool later," Adriana said. "It's not far from here. Now, *adelante!*"

The group followed. As Marlene happily talked to Adriana in Spanish, she managed to keep an eye on Sarita, who was striking up a conversation with Helen.

"We could have waited a couple minutes," said Sarita. "These people are so selfish!"

"I understand, though," Helen replied.

"It's their vacation. Not a big deal, anyway. He'll find us."

"I've been meaning to tell you — my friends and I follow the show, and we're very sorry you guys were voted out," Sarita said, blushing. "Your team was the best."

Helen smiled sadly. "That's nice of you, honey. I'm sorry it's over, too."

"Have you known Carloalberto for a long time?"

"Ah — only a few months. We only started working together on the show in January."

"Isn't he the most handsome guy in the world? A real king, isn't he?"

It was Helen's turn to blush.

"Oh, he —" she stuttered. "I suppose he isn't hard on the eyes."

Enough of this nonsense. Marlene took Sarita by the arm and steered her away from the screenwriter. "Sara Martínez!" she hissed.

"What? I wasn't doing anything wrong. You told me not to talk to Carloalberto, but you never said anything about Helen."

"All right, then. You stay away from *all* these people! They're trouble."

They walked to Mahahual, a small, tidy Costa Maya village with gift shops, bars, restaurants and an aviary. The pool was small but crystal clear. Everybody had a chance to greet Plato, a two-year-old dolphin with a wide smile that jumped through a hoop and "kissed" people. A resort photographer captured all their interactions — to later sell the pictures back to the guests. The whole thing lasted fifty minutes, and Carloalberto didn't end up making it.

After leaving the pool, Marlene and Sarita watched a sideshow of Mayan dancers spinning from tall poles. They visited the Fish Spa, where hungry goldfish nibbled at their toes. It tickled, but they left giggling and with smoother feet. Finally, they swung by a restaurant and grabbed some lobster tacos in jalapeño sauce. The waiter tried to get Marlene to order a Negra Modelo, but she refused. Taking care of Sarita made her feel like she was on duty, and she never drank on the job.

It wasn't noon yet, and Marlene had no desire to go back to the ship. She knew Sarita would start looking for Helen and Carloalberto the moment they were on board. There was an amusement park nearby, The Lost Mayan Kingdom, and she convinced her niece to explore it with her. After three hours on the water slides and splashing in the pools, Sarita seemed to have forgotten her crush and was her usual bubbly self.

When they returned to the North Star, tanned and tired, a documentary about aliens and the Chichen Itza pyramids was playing on the cabin TV. Sarita kicked off her shoes and plopped down on the sofa bed to watch.

"You think beings from another galaxy helped build the place we're going to see tomorrow?" she asked, wiggling her goldfish-nibbled toes.

"Sure, why not," Marlene said, relieved that Sarita had forgotten Carloalberto.

But two hours later, the name Carlos Alberto Casanova blared over the boat's loudspeakers. He was being called urgently to the Guest Services area. Sarita sat up.

"Did you hear that, Tía?"

"I did."

It was five twenty-five. The ship should have left for Cozumel at five, but they were still at the Costa Maya dock.

Another announcement came on after ten minutes, asking passengers to proceed immediately to their muster stations — the place where they had been instructed to meet in case of emergencies. Marlene and Sarita's muster station, where they'd stood around at the beginning of the trip during a mandatory drill, was outside the Forest Café.

The cabin attendant knocked on the door and they hurried outside.

"Is this another drill?" Marlene asked.

"No, ma'am, it's the real thing," the young man answered.

11: TWO WOMEN AND TWO STORIES

When the boat finally departed for Cozumel around seven o'clock that night, there was palpable tension. Though it hadn't been announced publicly, most passengers already knew, or at least suspected, that Carloalberto was missing.

Rumors ran wild after they were dismissed from their muster stations. Some people said the guy had just forgotten the time and kept drinking in one of the many Mahahual bars. Others believed he could've been assaulted, even kidnapped. Did those so-called "express kidnappings" still happen in the area? Those who knew about *The Terrific Two* suggested it was a publicity stunt.

"It would make sense," Sarita asserted. "Hollywood stars do that all the time. They come up with crazy ideas to get free press."

"But this wouldn't make him look very good," Marlene replied.

"So what? At least people would be talking about him. They already are, that's the point. In the meantime, he's having fun with the dolphins, off in a Mexican casino or drinking Negra Modelos and laughing it off. But he'll be back soon."

Sarita refused to believe that anything bad could've happened to her superstar. Marlene thought it was strange that the girl wasn't more concerned. Then she remembered that nobody, except for herself and the other woman who was out on the deck the night before, had heard the splash of something — someone? — into the water. She replayed the sound over and over in her head as hours passed.

Benito invited her to mojitos at The Ambassador bar during his only free time that day — thirty minutes before he reported for dinner duty at eight. He didn't seem worried either.

"This happens all the time, and the missing passengers always show up," he said. "They get sober and take a taxi to the next stop. Lucky for this *pendejo*, it's only a two-hour drive from Costa Maya to Cozumel."

Marlene didn't mention the splash. If Carloalberto was in fact off drunk or gambling somewhere, it would make her look paranoid — the cliché ex-cop. Besides, she and Benito had more interesting things to

86

talk about. He had already complimented her several times on her outfit, though he was never overtly flirtatious.

Later that evening, the captain released an official statement on video, acknowledging a passenger's "unexpected absence" and explaining that naval protocol had been followed. Mexican authorities had been notified, and the local police were looking for Carloalberto. A thorough search of the boat had been done, and he wasn't on board, but tips as to his whereabouts were welcome. Headshots of Carloalberto appeared on the ship's internal TV channel, followed by scenes from his *Terrific Two* reel and the telenovelas. Marlene didn't find him too convincing in any of his roles.

Without much else to do, those who were unfamiliar with the contest began Googling it with the slow and expensive onboard Internet connection. Helen and Emma were soon swamped by passengers wanting to help, chat or snoop.

Helen was willing to offer details. She had seen Carloalberto for the last time when he was gambling at the casino on the night of the dance.

"He was pretty upset after we were voted off the show," she said. "He pretended to be fine, but I didn't believe it for a second. We worked so hard!"

Emma refused to answer any questions. She asked to be left alone, which just fueled people's curiosity.

If this was, in fact, a publicity stunt, it had worked out quite well, Marlene conceded.

Helen also volunteered that Carloalberto had been suffering from depression, Sarita informed her aunt. The girl became increasingly agitated as the hours passed.

"Helen told me he was crushed when they lost," she said sadly. "But still, I don't think anything bad has happened, right, Tía?"

"Of course not."

"She's planning to give interviews to the Miami media once we reach Cozumel and have phone service. I can't wait to find out —"

Marlene didn't like that Sarita was talking to the screenwriter. But she couldn't very well forbid her niece from approaching Helen when so many other passengers were doing so. Unlike Emma, Helen didn't mind the attention. She even seemed to welcome it.

"You know what?" Sarita added. "Someone just found Carloalberto's phone in the casino. Now, *that's* scary. People don't just leave their phones when they get off a boat in a different country."

Despite Benito's reassurances, Marlene was nervous, too. That splash rang again in her ears, along with the *shamana*'s prophecy. *A blood trail.*

"But this one dissolves into the waves," she repeated.

If only to appease her conscience before bed, she requested a meeting with the staff captain, an affable-looking Dutch man she had seen mingling with the guests in the restaurants. When she told him about the noise, he didn't dismiss it, as she had feared he would. In fact, he admitted that three more passengers had reported hearing the splash.

"We're investigating it," he said in his slightly accented English. "We take our passengers' safety seriously here."

They arrived in Cozumel the following morning.

When passengers started getting off the boat at 8 A.M., a reporter from a Miami TV station was waiting outside. He shoved a microphone at Emma and asked where she thought her husband was.

"I have no idea," the model replied curtly.

"Did he sleep in your cabin the night before his disappearance?"

Emma looked like she wanted to slap the

interviewer, but she composed herself and said, "No. But it isn't uncommon for him to nap during the day and stay up all night. After all, we've been on vacation."

"Do you think he's still in Mahahual?"

"Most likely."

"Was he depressed after he and Ms. Hall were knocked out of the TV competition?"

"Not in the least. Carloalberto has been offered a role in a new movie and is looking forward to a new chapter in his career," she offered the camera with a courteous, professional smile. "I'm sure he's around somewhere. This is a minor incident that has been blown far out of proportion."

Upon hearing that, Sarita turned to her aunt and whispered, "Either she or Helen is lying."

Marlene nodded. Perhaps even both.

12: THE MAYAN BALL GAME

Marlene had booked herself and Sarita for an excursion called "Chichen Itza by Plane," which began with a fifty-minute flight from Cozumel to the ruins in an old Cessna Caravan. Only eight North Star passengers made the trip, which was pricey in itself — almost a thousand dollars per person. But Marlene had wanted to visit the area ever since she'd read José Martí's "The Indian Ruins" in *The Golden Age.*

"When that reporter left, Helen tried to talk to Emma, but Emma totally ignored her," Sarita told her as they flew over the Yucatán Peninsula. "So rude. She thinks she's better than everybody else just because she's been in *Vogue.* Actually, I'm not sure if it was *Vogue* or —"

"I wish you would stop involving yourself in these people's business," Marlene said. "You know what curiosity did to the cat."

Their tour guide, a fifty-something Mayan

archeologist with the nickname Turtle, was waiting for them at the entrance of the ruins. The place was already packed with tourists, so he led them briskly through the crowd.

"We need to make the most of these two hours," he said. "It's a pity that all of you aren't staying longer. We have some incredible light and sound shows at the pyramids at dusk."

Only two hours! Marlene hadn't realized that when she'd agreed to fork over handfuls of money. Chichen Itza, she thought, deserved more time.

Turtle took them first to the Great Ball Court, where the Mayans used to hold a ceremonial ball game called Pok-a-Tok. The field was rectangular, around five hundred feet long and two hundred feet wide. He showed them the sculpted panels at the base of the outer walls, which depicted two teams of players.

"Their goal was to toss the ball through a loop," he said, gesturing toward a stone hoop more than twenty feet off the ground on one side of the wall. "It was a solid rubber ball that weighed a good ten pounds. Players would hit it with their head, shoulders, hips or elbows, but they weren't allowed to use their hands or feet. Many were severely injured and even died after hitting the ball too hard with their head."

"I guess they didn't wear helmets back then," someone said.

"Actually, they did," Turtle said, pointing to a player on the wall panel with an elaborate headdress. "But we don't know how effective they were."

The games, Turtle went on as they walked around the grassy field, weren't for entertainment, but were considered religious events.

"Like football in Texas?" another tourist quipped.

"Sort of," Turtle answered. "But the outcome was quite different. Instead of being paid in shiny gold coins, players got a different kind of reward. The game was an offering to their gods, and when it was over, an entire team was offered to them as a sacrifice. And which one do you think they chose?"

"Obviously the losing team," Sarita said.

"No, Miss, they chose the winners," Turtle replied. "The Mayans believed in giving their gods only their best, most perfect offerings. Losers didn't qualify."

"Then I imagine both teams would try not to win," the girl replied.

"They fought with all they could to win,"

Turtle said. "For the Mayans, being sacrificed was the greatest honor a human could achieve. They believed that if they were offered up to the gods, they would live forever, and their names would be remembered for centuries."

They walked to El Caracol, a building that Turtle explained was known as "the observatory."

"The Mayans used to watch the sky from the top of the tower, without any trees or human structures obstructing the view."

The guide was still talking when Sarita cut him off, "Excuse me, Señor, but is it true that Chichen Itza was built with extraterrestrial help?"

"Some people say that," Turtle answered with a sly smile. "Skeletons with elongated skulls that don't look totally human have been found in this area." He produced the picture of a cone-headed skull and showed it to the group. "There is a theory that Quetzalcoatl, the feathered serpent god, was an alien that taught the Mayans astronomy and mathematics. After all, he's usually portrayed descending from the skies in a cloud of fire that *could* be a rocket."

"Oh, wow."

Afterward, they visited the Kukulkan pyramid — also known as El Castillo —

where people posed for the obligatory picture.

"During the spring and autumn equinox, the sun casts a shadow across the north face that looks like a serpent slithering down," Turtle said. "But there's more to it. Listen!"

He stood near the base of the pyramid and clapped his hands. The echo was an eerie chirping sound that took everybody by surprise.

"It's identical to the cry of the quetzal," he explained. "The Mayans considered these birds messengers of the gods."

At that moment, Sarita, who was looking at her phone, let out a loud shrill cry.

"What it is, *mija*?" Marlene asked.

"Carlo— Carloalberto," the girl said. "He's . . . dead."

Lips trembling, Sarita read a tweet from Univision News: "Body of missing North Star passenger recovered from the ocean off the Costa Maya waters this morning."

Other people took out their phones and began furiously Googling Carloalberto. Sarita was now crying hysterically.

Turtle approached them. "I'm so sorry. I've been following the news since yesterday. Did you know that gentleman?"

"No," Marlene answered.

"Yes," Sarita said at the same time. Then

her hand flew to her mouth and she quickly added, "I mean, no."

When Turtle led the group to the exit, everyone was quiet.

"The gods did take the best," Sarita mumbled, tears running down her face. "The most handsome and perfect one."

13: The Return Trip

In a subdued mood, the group boarded the bus that would take them back to the Chichen Itza airport. Sarita was searching the news frantically, her phone battery running low.

"Can I use yours, Tía? Please?" she asked.

"I left it on board. I didn't think we'd need it."

Sarita sighed in frustration and sat, sulking. Marlene took a seat next to the other woman who'd been smoking outside the night of the party. The woman recognized Marlene, too, and introduced herself as Lucy.

"I bet what we heard was that poor man jumping into the ocean," she said in hushed tones. "Isn't it terrible? I wish we'd said something then. Maybe someone could've saved him."

"I doubt they would've found him in the dark," Marlene answered. "But why do you think he jumped?"

"Oh," Lucy replied, "they found a recording. He left a final video message on his cell phone."

Sarita barged in on the conversation.

"Where did you hear that?" she asked urgently.

"On Univision," Lucy answered. "The video was posted there. It's heartbreaking."

Lucy pulled up the Univision website on her phone, but they were just streaming an interview with Helen. She was still at the Cozumel port, the North Star towering behind her.

"I've said it all along," the screenwriter said. "Carloalberto was depressed, no matter what *other people* claim. Yes, he'd been offered a new job on a feature film. And I was working on a pilot for the telenovela he was going to star in after that. But that doesn't mean we weren't devastated when —"

The Internet was slow even on Lucy's fully charged phone. The video stopped, Helen's face frozen, mouth open.

"There's zero doubt that he killed himself," Lucy explained to Sarita. "In the video, he said something like, 'Don't blame anybody. My life isn't worth living.' "

"But when did he record it?" the girl asked.

"I assume before jumping."

The bus had arrived at the airport. After all the passengers had boarded the Cessna Caravan, the pilot asked them to turn off their cell phones. Reluctantly, Lucy and Sarita obeyed, and moments later, the plane took off.

The sapphire waters of the Caribbean Sea gleamed below the plane. A few boats, like toy ships in a miniature lake, were eclipsed at times by the lacy veil of the clouds between. Marlene looked distractedly at them, but her mind wasn't there. It was back on the North Star. She had seen Carloalberto after he and Helen were knocked out of the contest — that evening on deck fifteen, when he was happily taking selfies with "his women." He didn't seem fazed, much less depressed. His own wife was saying he had been all right. So it was her word versus Emma's.

On the other hand, if Carloalberto *had* died the night of the party, and his body was what she had heard going overboard, he must have died shortly after Marlene had spotted him at the roulette table. He clearly owed money to some unsavory characters — speaking of which, where had that blond

99

guy been that night? Perhaps a streak of bad luck at the tables had driven Carloalberto over the edge.

Still, the time window was tight. He would've had to go to his room, shoot the video and make the jump in less than half an hour. Could he have been killed by one of "his women"? Emma, so cold and reserved? What if she *had* eventually caught him and Helen? Those two weren't exactly careful.

Sarita turned on her cell phone mid-flight. Marlene shot her a warning look.

"Sorry." The girl put the phone away.

"We'll be landing soon," Marlene said, "and then you can find out what's going on. We're almost there. See? That's the North Star."

The ship's brightly painted hull stood out among the other boats docked at the Cozumel port.

"This was supposed to be so much fun," Sarita said with a sad sigh. "Cruising the Caribbean with you, visiting cool places, sending pics to my friends. But now it's turned into a nightmare."

Marlene put a hand on her niece's shoulder. "Don't take it so hard, *mijita*," she said gently. "This is awful, yes, but you didn't know him."

"What do you mean? My friends and I have followed *The Terrific Two* since it first aired! And I was supposed to —" She stopped herself.

"Supposed to what?" Marlene asked, eyebrow raised. Perhaps Sarita would come forward about the WhatsApp group herself.

"Nothing," said Sarita, looking down.

Marlene put her arm around her niece. "I know you were rooting for him, but if he hadn't been on the cruise, this wouldn't have mattered as much to you," Marlene concluded. "It would've just been another piece of bad news."

"But he *was* here," Sarita answered.

14: Carloalberto's Last Video

From the Cozumel airport, the group took a bus back to the North Star. Alejandro Fernández was on the radio singing "El Rey." Thinking of her king, Sarita burst into tears.

"There, there," Lucy said, patting her on the back gently. "We all had a crush on him, didn't we?"

Marlene shot her a curious glance. *We all?*

"Damn right," Sarita sniffled.

During the ten-minute ride, thanks to Lucy and the other passengers, Marlene pieced together recent events. That morning, when checking her email for the first time in days, Emma noticed one from Carloalberto with a video attachment. "And there he was, my Carloalberto, saying that he was sorry for the pain he'd cause to those who loved him."

Emma stopped, her beautiful face grief-stricken. "It doesn't make sense. My husband was so happy-go-lucky. If being kicked out of the contest affected him that way, he never said so. In fact, when the last segments were being filmed, he told me was fed up with the whole thing and wanted to move on. He didn't care about that project anymore."

"I wonder what Helen will say now," Marlene whispered to Lucy.

"She's probably mad because the reporters aren't interviewing *her*," Lucy replied. "But some trip this has been, eh? This Chichen Itza excursion was highway robbery, if you ask me."

"Yeah, for the price, I expected at least half a day there," Marlene agreed.

"This whole cruise — I would've been better off staying home in Tucson. And I was so looking forward to my 'ocean view cabin,' but —" Lucy drew a cigarette out of her purse. Marlene did the same, and they began to smoke under the disapproving gaze of the other passengers. Some opened their windows, if only to make a statement, as the outside air was thick with exhaust fumes.

"But even *that* went wrong," Lucy continued. "The cabin was supposed to have a balcony, and I guess it does, technically, but there's a row of lifeboats in front of it blocking the view!"

"Yikes, sorry about that. Which deck are you on?"

"Twelve."

"We're on fourteen."

"Right above me, then — there's no deck thirteen on the North Star." Lucy chuckled. "Some kind of sailors' superstition, I guess."

"I didn't know that," Marlene said, realizing that Carloalberto and Emma must have been on deck twelve as well.

"Well, at least I got the cabin cheap," Lucy concluded. "This was my first cruise, and I didn't realize the fine print said 'partially obstructed view.' Well, you get what you pay for."

When they arrived at the dock, the reporters had already left. Marlene hoped for a reprieve from the whole Carloalberto affair, but as soon as they returned to their cabin, Sarita plugged her phone in to the charger and asked to borrow her aunt's.

"Can you give it a rest, *mijita*?"

"Tía, please! You know how important this is."

Marlene was too tired to argue. She retrieved the device from the depths of her purse and handed it to Sarita. After shaking her head at the cheap Motorola, the girl Googled Carloalberto's name and found the video. It was short, less than a minute, with the man's whole upper half onscreen.

"I'm addressing you all, dear ones, at the threshold of death. I'm sorry for the pain that my actions may cause you, but my life isn't worth living anymore, so I'm taking it. Don't blame anyone. *Adiós.*"

Carloalberto remained expressionless as he spoke. No emotion whatsoever in his voice or eyes.

"He sounds like he was reading off a piece of paper," Marlene said, having watched without much interest. "It just doesn't seem natural."

"How can you say that?" Sarita asked, horrified. "He was desperate!"

"But he doesn't look *desperate*," Marlene replied. "If anything, he looks bored."

"Shut up, Tía! Don't you have any respect for the dead?"

Then Marlene noticed something in the background. She asked Sarita to replay the video, watching attentively this time. The video had been filmed in one of the ship's cabins with Carloalberto's back to the balcony, an unobstructed view of the night behind him.

Marlene went outside, looked down and checked again the balcony where she had caught Carloalberto and Helen making out at the beginning of the trip. A compact row of lifeboats sat in front of it.

"He didn't film this in his cabin," she said to herself.

"What are you mumbling about?" Sarita asked.

"Nada," she said, not wanting to plant ideas in her niece's head.

The boat would stay in port until 5 P.M., when it would head back to Miami. Marlene wondered if she would have time to find out . . .

The captain's voice came through the loudspeakers, interrupting her thoughts.

"Those passengers who are currently in their staterooms must remain there until further instructions. Those who are anywhere else, proceed to your muster stations, where a crew member will be waiting for you. The Mexican police are coming aboard."

15: Cues from the Video

Marlene and Sarita lay around the cabin for the next two hours. In the meantime, Google News informed them that Emma was flying to Costa Maya to identify her husband's body.

"She'll have to make arrangements to take him home," Sarita said, blowing her nose. Her eyes were still red.

From their balcony they could see the dock, where three Mexican police cars waited near the ship.

"Does this have to do with Carloalberto?" Sarita asked. "If he killed himself, why are the cops here?"

Marlene could have explained to her niece that the suicide theory needed to be confirmed, but didn't want to rile the girl up again. She had rewatched the video a third time. While general consensus was that Carloalberto had placed his cellphone on a table and recorded himself, Marlene thought it looked as if someone was holding the phone and moving around a bit, creating a slight panning effect. At a certain point in the video, it slid so much to the left that the edge of a blue frame with a butterfly inside was visible for a few seconds.

Marlene glanced at the print that hung near their own balcony — it depicted a butterfly in a blue frame as well. For a fleeting second, she wondered if the video could have been shot in here, but knew the idea was absurd. All the cabins on the boat probably had the same framed prints.

Sarita pointed outside and yelled, "Look, Tía! There's the guy who was dancing with Emma the night of the party."

Fernando, now in handcuffs, was escorted out of the boat by four *federales.*

Marlene wondered why the Mexican cops hadn't interviewed the passengers or conducted a more thorough search of the boat. She was sure they hadn't been on her deck. How had they caught the guy so quickly?

Soon, the passengers were allowed to walk freely on board. The ship set sail. At 6 P.M., when the Cozumel coastline was only a thin blue line on the horizon, the captain made another public announcement on the ship's TV channel.

"On behalf of the North Star crew and

the entire company, we want to apologize to our guests for the inconveniences suffered during this trip. Though these regrettable events are due to circumstances outside our control, we understand that they have disrupted what should have been a pleasant experience. For this reason, we have decided to credit the accounts of each of our passengers with one thousand points, meaning one thousand dollars that can be applied toward any other cruise with our company."

The staff manager also made an appearance, explaining that the man arrested by the Mexican authorities was Pietro Monty, also known as Fernando Pedraza. Emma had accused him of running illicit gambling rings in Florida and blackmailing her late husband, which might have driven him to his death. She had reported him to the police as soon as she left the boat.

Marlene met Benito before his evening shift. He agreed that the *federales* had done a quick-and-dirty job.

"They arrested what's-his-name because Emma tipped them off," Benito said. "They couldn't very well ignore threats. But other than that . . ."

Marlene nodded.

"I've been thinking about it, and you know what? I don't believe they care about

111

this. It happened at sea, not in their jurisdiction, and they'd rather not make a big deal out of something that could hurt tourism."

"Yep, our *federales* have more to worry about than onboard crimes," Benito said. "Better for them to let the American police deal with that. Now, for something a little more pleasant. Can you guess tonight's featured main course at The Ambassador?"

Marlene waited, batting her eyelashes in mock ignorance.

"A very Cuban dish," he said. *"Ropa vieja."*

"Ooh." Shredded beef, one of her favorites. "Did you use tomato paste?"

"Goya tomato paste. I happened to have some in stock."

"What are you serving it with?"

"White rice and fried plantains."

"Perfect," Marlene chuckled. "Can't wait to see Sarita's face when she's presented with a dish called 'old clothes.'"

They had a nice time together, as usual, but after Benito left, Marlene stayed. She just couldn't get Carloalberto's death out of her mind. The suicide theory made sense, given his obvious gambling problem and the threats she'd overheard at the start of the trip. But that last video bothered her. Where had it been shot, if not Carloalberto and Emma's cabin? Marlene pondered whether it was worth finding out, and ultimately decided it was.

You are a natural-born bloodhound and will soon follow another trail.

This was their last full day at sea; they would arrive in Miami the next morning at six o'clock. If Marlene was going to do some digging, she only had the evening for it. But how would she occupy Sarita? She certainly didn't want her niece tagging along with her for this.

Her answer came when the "last and best sale of the cruise" was announced at 7:30 P.M. Marlene sent the girl straight to the boutiques with her credit card.

"Buy yourself something nice, *mijita,* but don't you spend over fifty dollars," she said.

Sarita pranced off.

It was about the time when the room attendants made their pre-dinner rounds to make the beds for the night and tidy up the cabins. Marlene knew that they usually worked on several staterooms at once, leaving the doors open while vacuuming to move between them faster. She hung out by the elevators, keeping an eye on the cleaning crew.

Most rooms were empty. Not only was the "awesome sale" going on, but a Cirque du Soleil show — the only one of the cruise —

had begun. A young man began knocking on doors. If no one answered, he swiped in and began to vacuum, leaving the door open behind him so he could change the linens.

As soon as he opened Helen's cabin door, Marlene hid around the corner and waited. When the attendant left it open and moved to the next, she went quietly inside.

16: POETIC JUSTICE

Her first glance was to a print of a butterfly in a blue frame on the wall next to the balcony door. So all the stateroom rooms did look exactly the same — two beds, a dresser, an armchair and a big closet. Marlene opened the closet doors and saw only a few dresses and a pair of jeans. A silver tray and two glasses sat at the minibar, but her trained eyes noticed the absence of the stainless-steel carafe.

She proceeded to the dresser and, as silently as she could, opened the first drawer. A leather-bound journal was inside. The first page read: *Love Gone Wrong.* A pilot for a miniseries. *Synopsis: Antonio, a philandering, too-handsome-for-his-own-good rapper, leaves a series of spurned lovers in his wake. But when he's rejected by the one woman he truly falls for, he despairs and eventually commits suicide."*

Marlene began leafing through the journal's handwritten pages — fortunately, Helen's penmanship was easy to read.

The characters, of course, were familiar: Antonio was a poorly disguised version of Carloalberto. There was a mean, pretty fashion icon standing in for Emma, who had been demoted in the script from wife to one of the protagonist's many girlfriends. Another character was an enigmatic older woman who Marlene assumed was Helen herself.

The script was middling, but Marlene wanted to finish it anyway. She considered taking it to her cabin when a page caught her attention. Some lines were underlined in red:

Antonio (looks at the camera with a gun in his hand): I'm addressing you all, dear ones, at the threshold of death. I'm sorry for the pain that my actions may cause you, but my life isn't worth living anymore, so I'm taking it. Don't blame anyone.

Adiós.

"What are you doing here?"

Marlene spun around. Helen was standing behind her, wrapped in a purple sarong and dripping, just back from the pool. She grabbed the journal from Marlene and shot toward the balcony.

But Marlene reacted quickly, back to her former self as a Cuban Revolutionary Police lieutenant. She forced Helen against a wall and recovered the journal.

"I'm going to call security!" the screen-writer said unconvincingly.

"Yes, why don't you?" Marlene shrugged. "Save me the trouble. They'll be happy to find Carloalberto's killer."

Helen walked to the door. She hesitated, then looked back.

"I have no idea what you mean. And why do you care anyway?"

"I don't, really," Marlene admitted. "But," she pointed to the underlined words. "his last words. A pretty strange coincidence, isn't it?"

"I wrote that long before Carloalberto died," Helen said. "I'd even shown this to him. The fact that it *did* end up happening that way was almost poetic justice."

"Poetic justice," Marlene repeated. "That's a couple of big Sunday words to describe what you did. You had him read from your script, took a recording and killed him. It's as clear as the Cozumel waters you threw his body into."

A room attendant came in. "Oh, pardon

me," he said on seeing the two of them. "I'll be back later."

He slipped out, closing the door behind him.

"Look, I can explain everything," Helen said.

Marlene settled down on one bed, keeping the journal out of Helen's reach. She knew it wasn't the best idea to sit in a locked room with a stone-cold killer, but the attendants were right outside, and Marlene would raise hell if Helen even got close to her. And besides, it was highly unlikely the woman could be hiding a weapon under that wet sarong.

"Go ahead," she said.

Helen sat on the other bed, facing Marlene.

"Carloalberto and I have known each other a long time," she said. "Long before he was famous — or almost famous. He's always been a smug bastard, but I still fell for him."

Like Marlene had fallen for Yoel.

"I kept trying to protect him, giving him money to get him out of trouble because he's — was a compulsive gambler. I must have loaned him over ten thousand dollars that he never intended to pay back."

There was a pause. Marlene gazed out the

glass balcony door. No land in sight. The ship seemed perfectly suspended between sea and sky.

"So you killed him over a few thousand dollars?" she prodded.

"No, no! I was working on that script — the one in the notebook — for a contest like the one we lost and needed an actor to read from a scene. I asked Carloalberto to record it on his phone since mine was gone."

"I remember."

Helen's voice wavered. "You must think I'm so silly. He probably did, too. The night of the party, after he'd maxed out his credit card in the casino, he finally agreed to do me this favor. We were friends, after all."

"Not just friends," Marlene corrected.

Helen's cheeks turned red. "No, much more,' " she said. "We met right when he'd arrived from Cuba. I was his first American girlfriend, and I was devastated when he left me for Emma. But then he came back, begging for forgiveness. He said he wanted to finance his own movie. It's time-consuming and expensive to do. I put a second mortgage on my house so we could start production and find co-sponsors. We never got them, and I — I lost my home."

Heat flared on Marlene's cheeks, too. She felt a pang of empathy from the corner of her heart that still grieved for her mother's house.

"When we teamed up for the contest, he made me lie about our story," Helen went on. "He wanted to pretend it was the beginning of our collaboration. He got back together with Emma and proposed right away, 'for publicity,' he swore, even though it was clear she really loved him."

"He really got away with that?" Marlene asked.

"She was already famous, and their marriage did actually give us a leg up on the show. Of course he was in love with her, not me, and I refused to see it." Tears began to trickle down Helen's face. She wiped them away. "He kept saying I was 'the one.' And I would've believed anything, coming from him."

The ship lurched. High waves, uncommon in the summer, began to rock it back and forth.

"What I don't understand," Marlene said, "is why you took this trip knowing he would be here with his wife. It makes it seem like you were stalking him."

Helen blinked. "No! In fact, he was the one who persuaded me to come on this cruise. I wanted to move on and forget him. But he was so convinced we would win the competition that he insisted I come with him and Emma. If the two of us were aboard when the winners were announced, we'd get amazing press. The cruise company might even offer us a sponsorship, or him and Emma a contract for a couple of commercials. He was always thinking along career lines. I should've known better, though. He wasn't a great actor. We only managed to stay on the show that long because of his looks."

Marlene nodded. "His 'farewell speech' certainly wasn't too convincing."

Helen threw her hands in the air. "Tell me about it! That was the crappiest acting I've seen in years. He was drunk by then. So was I, by the way. I'd had one too many during that silly party and I was . . . not thinking clearly, I guess. When he finished recording, I tried to ask him about us. Absurdly, after all that time, I'd still held out hope that we had a shot. That I hadn't ruined my life for nothing. In response, he just asked if I could help him pay his debts one last time. 'La Eme is after me,' he said. The Mexican mafia, serious stuff."

"Were you planning to bail him out again?" Marlene asked.

"I didn't have the money for it." Helen put her head in her hands. "I begged him to tell me if our relationship had a chance. He laughed. 'Relationship? Your only relationship with me is as my screenwriter. And you suck at it, writing this stupid script about kings and knights! You couldn't have done a little better?' " Helen was crying again.

"He put the blame on *me* for losing! After everything I'd sacrificed for him. He turned to leave, and I was so furious that I took the water jug and hit him in the head."

Marlene pictured an enraged Helen going after her former lover with the stainless-steel carafe. It almost made her laugh.

"But that alone wouldn't have killed him," she said.

"No, it only dazed him. But he was already drunk. He fell down and banged his head on the door. Passed out immediately. I started to think about what would happen if he was found wounded or unconscious in my cabin. All the explaining I'd have to do! And how he'd treated me — I was done. Had I been sober, I would never have . . . I'm not a violent person, no matter what you might think."

Helen stopped and shook her head slowly, as if processing what she'd just said herself. Then she went on in a hoarse voice. "I dragged him to the balcony and threw him overboard, then the water jug after him. I knew Emma wouldn't look for him until morning, since he spent half his nights in the casino."

Marlene inhaled loudly and asked, "Was it then that you decided to try to make it look like a suicide?"

"Not right away. It wasn't until later that night. I'd kept his phone, and there was the recording. It was a godsend. The timetables weren't perfect, but I hoped no one would notice. I sent off an email with the video attachment to Emma from his account. To go with it, I wrote something pretty close to what he'd said in the video."

"What did you do with the phone after that?"

"I wiped it down and dropped it by the roulette table when we came back from the dolphin excursion. Someone returned it to Emma. In the meantime, I told everybody he'd been depressed. Even Emma accepted it after seeing the email."

Helen seemed sad, but not particularly remorseful. Marlene peered into her eyes.

"Do you resent Emma?" she asked.

Helen sighed. "Of course I hated her at first. I saw her as the woman who stole Carloalberto from me. But then I found out he'd cheated — was still cheating — on both of us with so many other women. She never suspected it — she's way too naïve. I ended up feeling sorry for her. And I know she loved him. She must be devastated right now. But she's young and beautiful and has so much going for her. I think he would've ruined her life, too."

Helen fell silent. Marlene thought of Yoel again and looked at the screenwriter. As a police officer, she would never, ever have empathized with a criminal like this, but she wasn't a detective anymore. She had left that life behind on the island, along with her uniform and her old Makarov. Now, she was the owner and manager of La Bakería Cubana, anxious to return to her oven and storefront. And her dog, Max, who would never betray her.

"One last thing, Helen," she said softly. "Why in the world did you keep this journal? It's damning, even you must know that."

"I didn't think there would be a search," Helen answered. "Even if they didn't believe it was suicide, Carloalberto has so many unpaid debts to dangerous people. And . . . well, I just couldn't let that one last piece of him go."

"I'm afraid you'll have to."

"What do you mean?"

Marlene stood up and walked to the

balcony. Helen followed. The waters were choppy, and the wind had picked up. Marlene threw the journal into the ocean.

"*Adiós,* Carloalberto," she said.

EPILOGUE

The North Star was finally docked in the Miami port. It was nine-thirty; disembarkation was scheduled for ten. Marlene lingered on the promenade deck, watching Sarita, who was busy snapping pictures of the Miami skyline. But her heart, her aunt noticed, wasn't in it. This murder business must have been hard on her. With any luck, her grief would be short-lived. Most things were, at that age. Marlene hoped she'd soon have another crush to obsess over.

Speaking of crushes — where was Benito? Marlene had hoped to see him again before leaving the ship, but told herself she didn't care. He hadn't gone out of his way to find her, and anyway, he was just an acquaintance, someone she would probably never see again. She had real life to think about now.

The memory of her conversation with Helen and the discarding of the notebook

127

haunted Marlene. How could it not? Her former homicide-detective self bucked against letting the screenwriter get away with literal murder, but the scorned woman in her gleefully approved of it.

Sarita joined her, still looking downcast. Marlene put an arm around her.

"You okay?" she asked softly.

"Yeah, but I have to rethink my future. I wouldn't make a very good journalist," Sarita said.

"Oh?" Marlene raised an eyebrow. "And why's that? From what I understand, you did quite well at your internship with the *Journal*."

"It's a long story." Sarita fiddled with her phone case until the glitter started to rub off. "Jane, Lupe and I have this online newspaper. It was just a class project at first, but we kept it going. I was supposed to interview Carloalberto for a big feature. But now it's too late — I've let the girls down."

Marlene held back laughter at her paranoid suspicions about what the three of them had been up to. "You can still do your feature, *mijita*. Instead of an interview, just write about what happened. 'Aspiring actor's mysterious death on cruise,' or something like that. What's the saying? If it bleeds, it leads, right?"

As Sarita considered the idea, her eyes brightened.

"Okay," she said. "But instead of 'aspiring,' I'll say 'famous.' Or just 'actor.' In this business, you have to be careful with adjectives."

"Hola, chicas!" said a voice behind them. "I've been looking for you all over the place."

There was Benito, carrying a round cardboard box. He tipped an imaginary hat to Sarita and handed the box to Marlene.

"From one baker to another," he told her. "A culinary souvenir."

Marlene blushed. Sarita grinned and muttered something about eggs needing salt.

"Thank you," Marlene said. "What is it?"

"A fresh bonbon cake."

The box was wrapped with a red ribbon, tied into a lush bow on top.

"This is so sweet of you, Benito."

She gave him her business card from La Bakería Cubana. Benito looked at it and put it in his pocket. "I'll be visiting very soon."

"And I'll present you with my very own version of this cake."

Disembarkation was underway. Five thousand travelers left their staterooms, their pools, their casinos, their open bars. While awaiting her turn, Marlene saw Helen approach the walkway with a genuine smile on her face and a lightness in her step and wondered how many other illegal acts had gone unremarked during that short cruise. After all, what could be expected from such a crowd in close quarters but shenanigans?

ABOUT THE AUTHOR

Teresa Dovalpage was born in Havana and now lives in Hobbs, where she is a Spanish and ESL professor at New Mexico Junior College. She has published nine novels and three collections of short stories. Her English-language novels are *A Girl like Che Guevara* (Soho Press, 2004), *Habanera, a Portrait of a Cuban Family* (Floricanto Press, 2010), and *Death Comes in Through the Kitchen* (Soho Crime, 2018), a culinary mystery with authentic Cuban recipes.